# ACORN WAS A LITTLE WILD

Written by JEN ARENA    Illustrated by JESSICA GIBSON

SCHOLASTIC INC.

# ACORN

was a wild little thing,
pointy on one end and
capped on the other.

He was the first
of his generation to
jump off the tree.

"Don't do that," said Oak. "Squirrels will get you."

"I don't care about squirrels," said Acorn. "I just want to ROLL."

And roll he did.

He liked the feel of the
sun on his face and the
wind against his cap.

He even took
to taunting the
squirrels.

Nah-
nah - nah - nah-
nah!

Sure enough, just as Oak
had warned, a squirrel got him.
She scooped Acorn into her paws
and scrambled up a tree.

And Acorn loved it, because
Acorn was a wild little thing.
He loved the thrill of the climb
and the kick of bounding
from branch to branch.

Then the squirrel took a nibble of Acorn.

Acorn did NOT love that.

Whoa, whoa, whoa!
Wait a minute there,
buddy!

Before the squirrel could nibble more, a dog came along. And the dog and the squirrel barked back and forth until the squirrel forgot all about Acorn and dropped him.

And the rush, man, the rush of falling from the tree!
It was even better than when Acorn
had jumped that first time from Oak.

Acorn hit the ground and rolled down the hill again.

He sat in the grass for days and days, and the rain came and pounded on his shell like a good Swedish massage, and Acorn loved that, because Acorn was wild that way.

Eventually, another squirrel found Acorn.
"Let's go, go, GO!" Acorn cheered.
"I want to feel the wind against my cap!"

But the squirrel didn't carry him up a tree.

The squirrel took Acorn
and buried him
deep in the ground.

And that was no fun at all.

But after a while,
Acorn noticed cool
things going on
down there.

The worms were so chill,
wiggling around and
tickling him as they
passed, and Acorn
laughed when they did,
because even underground,
Acorn was still a little wild.

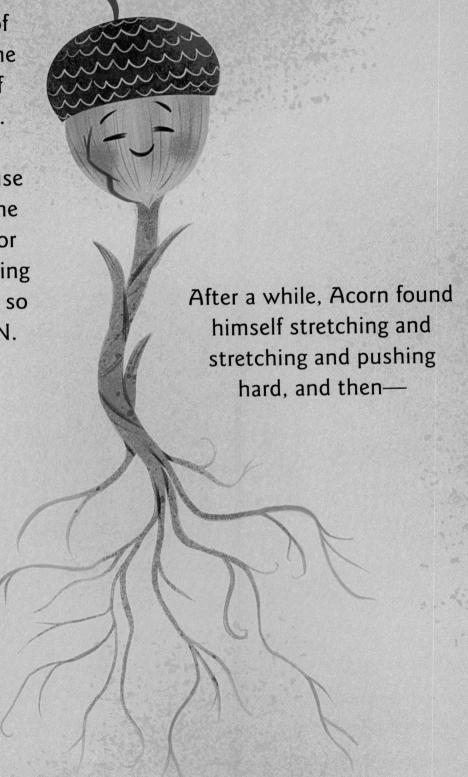

Acorn had a lot of time to think in the dark. He felt as if he was changing. He didn't quite understand, because he'd been the same wild little acorn for so long. But changing was an adventure, so Acorn was ALL IN.

After a while, Acorn found himself stretching and stretching and pushing hard, and then—

He felt the sun for the first time in ages.
Acorn had grown out of his cap and
popped right up through the ground.
And it was SO COOL.

He liked it so much,
he put down a few
more roots and
kept on growing.

Day after day,

week after week,

month after month,

year after year.

Acorn hadn't lost his wild side. Sometimes
he shook his leaves after a summer storm and
rumble-laughed when the squirrels got all wet.

Dink.

And if a fox peed on his trunk?
He dropped a stick on its noggin.

He never told another acorn,
"Don't do that." He always
said, "Go for it!"

And when the sun was low and the moon was high and the owls hooted in the night, he called all his friends together.

And he loved every minute.
Because Acorn was an oak . . .

but still a little wild inside.

For Katherine and Evelyn.
May you grow into mighty oaks.
—J. A.

For my loving, supportive family.
—J. G.

ISBN 978-1-339-03445-4

12 11 10 9 8 7 6 5 4 3 2 1                                   23 24 25 26 27 28

Printed in the U.S.A.                                              40

First Scholastic printing, September 2023

The text for this book was set in ITC Goudy Sans.
The illustrations for this book were rendered digitally in Photoshop and with a Wacom tablet.